Myrtle Swims Home

by B.T. Scherer

Edited by
James Stevick

Myrtle Swims Home

This book is written to provide information and motivation to readers. Its purpose is not to render any type of psychological, legal, or professional advice of any kind. The content is the sole opinion and expression of the author, and not necessarily that of the publisher.

Copyright © 2025 by B.T. Scherer.

Printed in the United States of America.

ISBN   978-1-64552-268-3   (Paperback)
ISBN   978-1-64552-270-6   (Hardback)
ISBN   978-1-64552-269-0   (Digital)

Lettra Press books may be ordered through booksellers or by contacting:

Lettra Press LLC
30 N Gould St. Suite 4753
Sheridan, WY 82801
1 307-200-3414 | info@lettrapress.com
www.lettrapress.com

For
Myrtle

Look out there! It's Myrtle,
the Loggerhead sea turtle.
In the ocean, big and wide,
Myrtle is swimming with the tide.

She flaps her flippers.
Watch her glide!

Myrtle swims up
from the ocean bed.
At the surface,
she pops up her head.

Her shell is yellow,
brown and red.

The sea current is flowing,
and the moon is glowing
Where is Myrtle going?

Myrtle is swimming home,
resting and gliding
through the sea foam.

She is hoping to reach,
the very same beach,
where she was born.

What will she do there?
She will lay her eggs with care.

How many eggs will there be?
Oh! Eighty, ninety,
or a hundred and three.

Goodness gracious, golly gee!
So many! How can that be?

When do baby turtles hatch?
Would you like to know?
It takes sixty days or so.

They peck through the white eggshell,
then they crawl to the surface,
going pell-mell.

Myrtle swims up to the surface,

takes a breath and resubmerges.

How far has she come?
Over six thousand miles,
and then some.

Does she rest along the way?
Yes, sometimes at night,
and sometimes in the day.
EUROPE
SPAIN
AFRICA
SARGASSO
SEA
FLORIDA
TH
CA

Oh my! What is all the commotion,
in the ocean?

It's Porpie, the porpoise,
flipping and jumping high.
Many friends are passing by,
waving and shouting "Hi, Hi, Hi!"

The bluefish, and the red snapper,
are both looking dapper.

The French angel, and the high hat,
are not so fat.

The stingray says,
"Have a nice day!"

The moray eel
   asks, "How do you feel?"

The sea star,
   can't go far.

The sand dollar,
   likes to holler

The jelly fish,

sends a birthday wish.

The sand flea,

invites Myrtle to tea.

And all of them,

live happily in the sea.

"Hello, Porpie,

come join me.

Let's swim together

hap-pi-ly."

Porpie, the Porpoise,

does a flip.

Then he joins Myrtle

on her trip.

Swimming together

in the Gulf Stream,

Porpie and Myrtle

make a good team.

"My instinct guides me to the beach.
Where the sand is golden, and the sky is blue.
I return every other year, as I always do.
I lay my eggs in the same place, too.

"And there is another reason
I want you to know.
It is about my birth on the beach,
so many years ago.
It was turtle-hatching season,
and the moon was aglow.

"It was time for me to hatch,
to break free,
begin to scratch.

But I was stuck inside my shell.
It was dark,
and it was still.

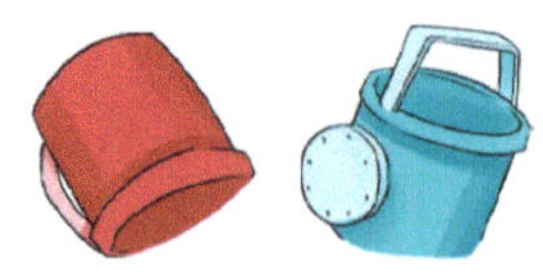

"Suddenly, I felt a gentle hand

of someone digging

in the sand.

A little girl scooped me up,

and carried me home

in a teacup.

"The little girl was named Bee-tee,
    and her big brother was Char-ley.
Together, they took care of me
    in a large aquarium by the sea.

"Every day they fed me fish.
    And tiny shrimp made a tasty dish.
I grew big and strong, you know.
    Then one night, they let me go.

"I wiggled down the beach.
The full moon was high,
shining above in the sky.

I felt the cool water
under my shell.
Feeling the ocean
was a thrill!

"Now I am grown,
    and a mother myself.
Leaving behind
    the coral shelf.

I'll lay my eggs,
    then back to sea
knowing my babies
    safe will be.

"Porpie, Porpie,
give a cheer.
We made it.
We are here!

Good-bye, Porpie,
my dear friend.
Come back soon
to swim again."

Myrtle the Sea Turtle

has swum home.

She has crawled out

from the foam.

She will dig her nest
and crawl around,
to lay her eggs
so small and round.

Myrtle has swum home again!
It's time for our story to end.

Goodbye, Myrtle, our ocean friend.
Be safe until we meet again.

The End

... but wait, there's more...

The ocean is big.

The ocean is wide.

Baby turtles love to hide.

Can you count them?
Golly gee,
How many turtles,
do you see?